# GRANDMA'S PEAR TREE
## EL PERAL DE ABUELA

WRITTEN BY / ESCRITO POR SUZANNE SANTILLAN
ILLUSTRATED BY / ILUSTRADO POR ATILIO PERNISCO

*To my family and friends, thanks for helping me make a dream come true.*  *SS*

*I dedicate this book to all the children I know—the kids from Coolidge, Child's Garden,
the Pasqualers, the Miclat kids, Alex, Briana, Seba, Claudita, Andrew, Gabriel, and Anthony.
And, most importantly, my own and dearest Camilu.*  *AP*

Text ©2010 Suzanne Santillan
Illustration ©2010 Atilio Pernisco
Translation ©2010 Raven Tree Press

Santillan, Suzanne.

    Grandma's pear tree / written by Suzanne Santillan; illustrated by Atilio Pernisco; translated
by Cambridge BrickHouse = El peral de Abuela / escrito por Suzanne Santillan; ilustrado por
Atilio Pernisco;  traducción al español de Cambridge BrickHouse —1 ed. —McHenry, IL :
Raven Tree Press,  2010.

    p.;cm.

    SUMMARY: A ball gets stuck in Grandma's pear tree and
               everyone in the family tries to help get it back.

Bilingual Edition
ISBN 978-1-934960-80-6 hardcover
ISBN 978-1-934960-81-3 paperback

English-only Edition
ISBN 978-1-934960-82-0 hardcover

    Audience: pre-K to 3rd grade
    Title available in English-only or bilingual English-Spanish editions

1. Family/Multigenerational—Juvenile fiction. 2. Lifestyles/Country Life—Juvenile fiction.
3. Bilingual books—English and Spanish. 4. [Spanish language materials—books.]
I. Illust. Pernisco, Atilio.  II. Title. III. Title: El peral de Abuela.

LCCN:  2009931226

Printed in Taiwan
10 9 8 7 6 5 4 3 2 1
First Edition

**Raven Tree Press**
A Division of Delta Systems Co., Inc.
www.raventreepress.com

**Free activities for this book are available at www.raventreepress.com**

PRINTED WITH
SOY INK

# GRANDMA'S PEAR TREE

# EL PERAL DE ABUELA

WRITTEN BY / ESCRITO POR SUZANNE SANTILLAN

ILLUSTRATED BY / ILUSTRADO POR ATILIO PERNISCO

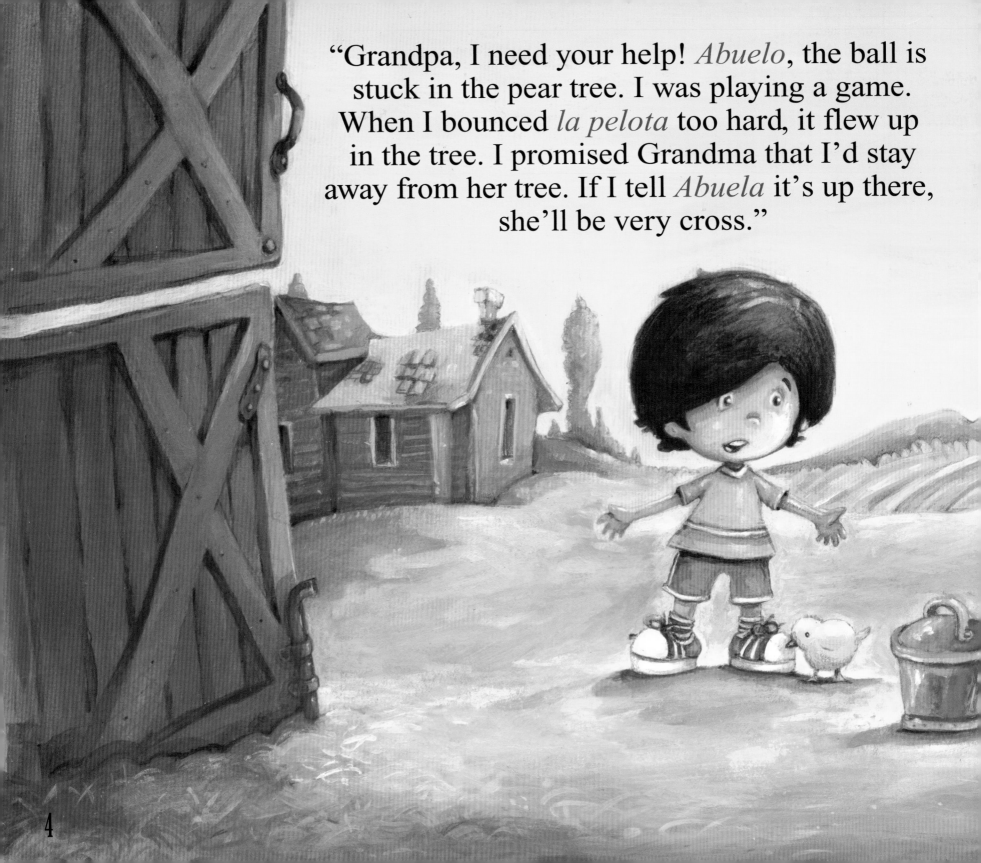

"Grandpa, I need your help! *Abuelo*, the ball is stuck in the pear tree. I was playing a game. When I bounced *la pelota* too hard, it flew up in the tree. I promised Grandma that I'd stay away from her tree. If I tell *Abuela* it's up there, she'll be very cross."

"I must finish milking the cow," *Abuelo* replied. "Throw your shoe at it. *El zapato* may get it down. When I'm done milking *la vaca*, I will help you."

Jessie walked up to *Abuela's* pear tree and threw his *zapato*…

"Oh no! *¡Ay, caramba!*"

7

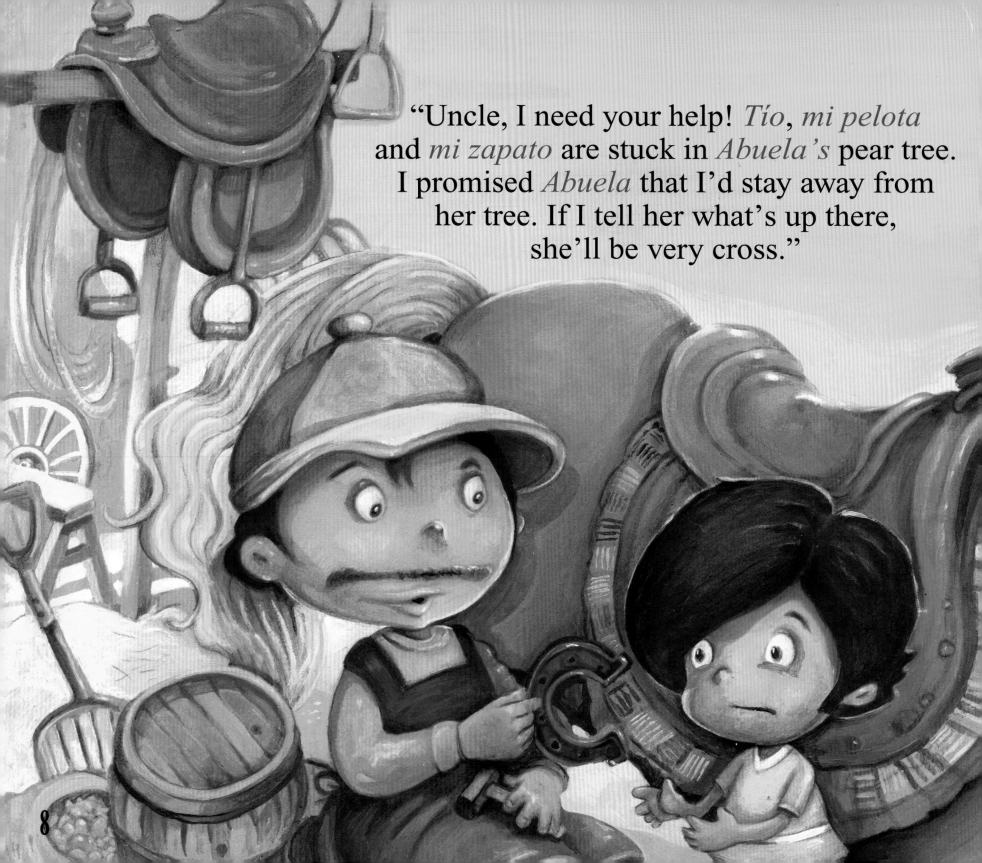

"Uncle, I need your help! *Tío*, *mi pelota* and *mi zapato* are stuck in *Abuela's* pear tree. I promised *Abuela* that I'd stay away from her tree. If I tell her what's up there, she'll be very cross."

"The horse needs
a new shoe," *Tío* replied.
"Use the broom.
*La escoba* may get
them down.

When I'm done
shoeing *el caballo*,
I will help you."

9

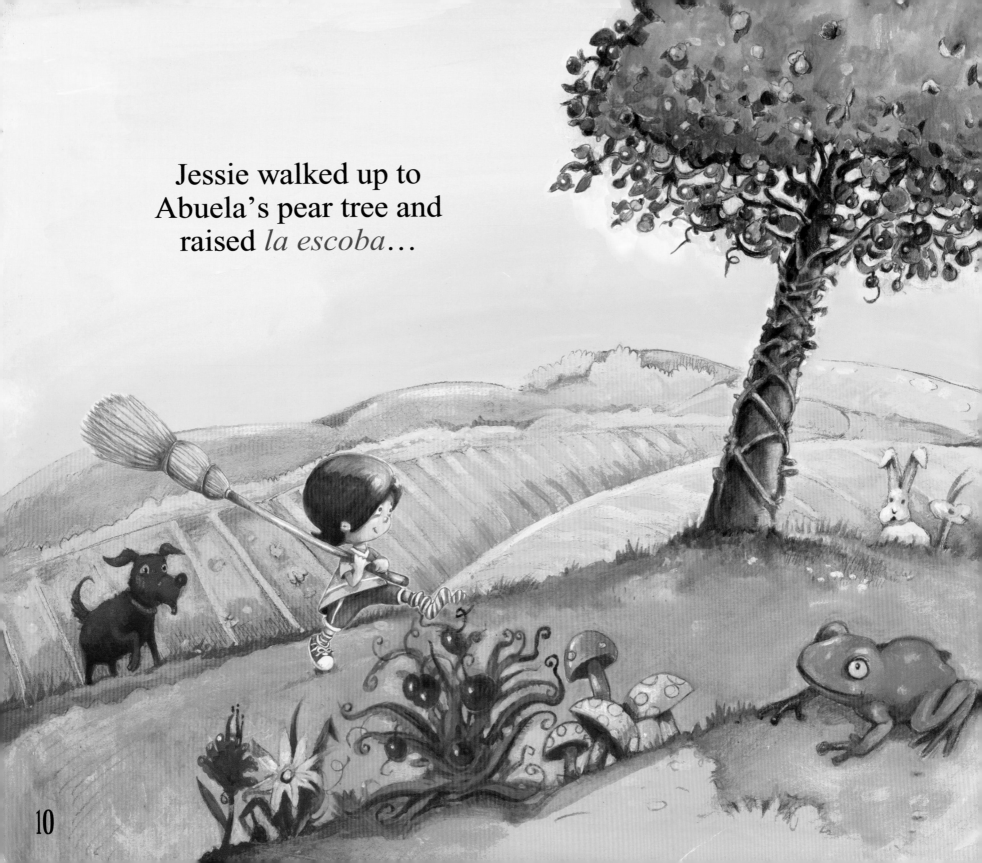

Jessie walked up to Abuela's pear tree and raised *la escoba*…

10

"Oh no! *¡Ay, caramba!*"

11

"Cousin, I need your help! *Primo*,
*mi pelota*, *mi zapato* and *la escoba*
are stuck in *Abuela's* pear tree.

I promised *Abuela* that I'd stay away from her tree.
If I tell her what's up there, she'll be very cross."

"The goat has escaped from his pen," *Primo* replied. "Use the chicken.

*El pollo* will fly in the tree and knock your things down. When I've caught *el chivo*, I will help you."

Jessie walked up to *Abuela's* pear tree and tossed *el pollo*…

14

"Oh no! *¡Ay, caramba!*"

15

"Sister, I need your help! *Hermana*, *el pollo*, *la escoba*, *mi zapato*, and *mi pelota* are stuck in *Abuela's* pear tree. I promised *Abuela* that I'd stay away from her tree. If I tell her what's up there, she'll be very cross."

"The donkey needs water and food," *Hermana* replied.
"Use the cat. *El gato* will scare *el pollo*. The flapping
and squawking will knock your things down. When
I am done feeding *el burro*, I will help you."

Jessie brought *el gato* to *Abuela's* pear tree.
He climbed to a very tall branch…
and lay down to sleep.

18

"Oh no! *¡Ay, caramba!*"

19

"*Abuela*, I'm sorry. I broke my promise to you.
But it all started with *la pelota*…"

20

"Oh little one, I'm not cross with you," *Abuela* replied. "Family is more important than even my tree."

"I have an idea," said *Abuela* as she looked
at the things stuck up in her tree.

"Let's get the ladder. *La escalera* is very heavy, but if you help me, we can lift it together."

*Abuela* climbed up to the top of her tree and started dropping the things down.

Down walked *el gato* as calm as can be.

Down flew *el pollo*.

25

Down dropped *la escoba*.

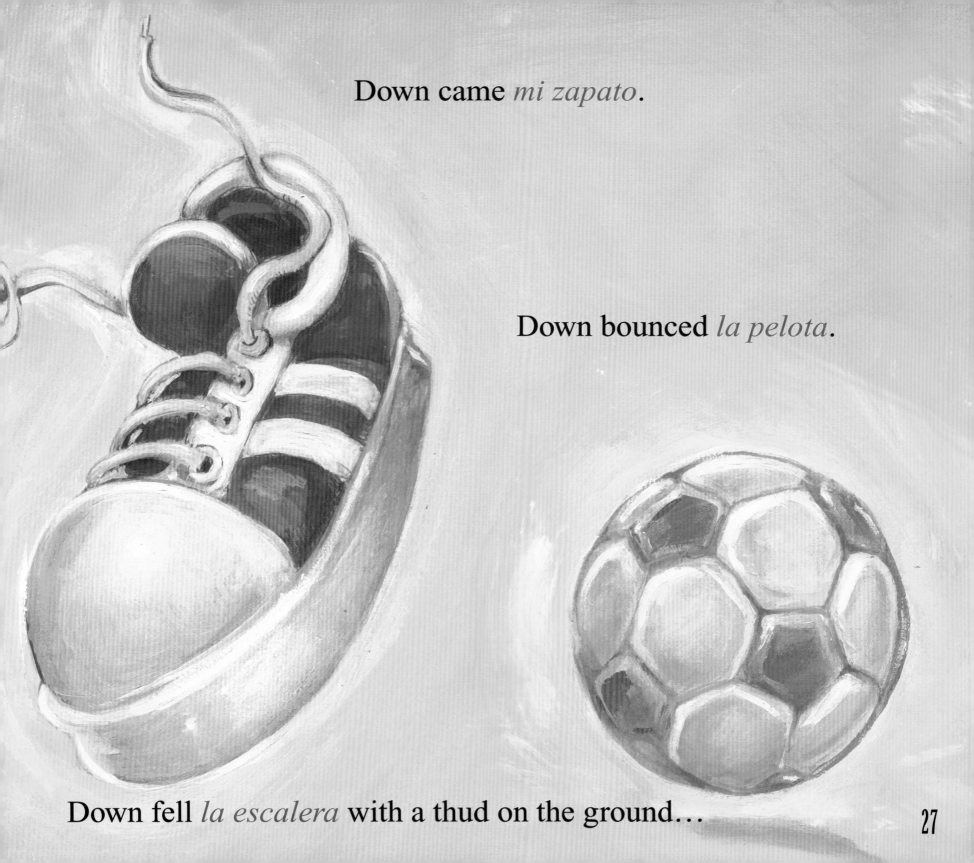

Down came *mi zapato*.

Down bounced *la pelota*.

Down fell *la escalera* with a thud on the ground...

27

"Oh my! *¡Ay, chihuahua!*"

28

"Everyone, come quickly! Now *Abuela* is stuck in her tree!"

30

# Vocabulary / Vocabulario

| | |
|---|---|
| grandpa | el (los) abuelo(s) |
| ball | la(s) pelota(s) |
| grandma | la(s) abuela(s) |
| shoe | el (los) zapato(s) |
| cow | la(s) vaca(s) |
| Oh no! | ¡Ay, caramba! |
| uncle | el (los) tío(s) |
| broom | la(s) escoba(s) |
| horse | el (los) caballo(s) |
| cousin | el (los) primo(s) |
| chicken | el (los) pollo(s) |
| goat | el (los) chivo(s) |
| sister | la(s) hermana(s) |
| cat | el (los) gato(s) |
| donkey | el (los) burro(s) |
| ladder | la(s) escalera(s) |
| Oh my! | ¡Ay, chihuahua! |